A Most Extraordinary Form of Animal

A Short Story of Time Travel

Ian Roberts

© 2018

Deeper Realms Book 1

Books by Ian Roberts

Deeper Realms 1 – A Most Extraordinary Form of Animal

Deeper Realms 2 – Unconfirmed Sighting

Deeper Realms 3 – Last Known Outbreak

Deeper Realms 4 – Valley of Dry Bones

For Flash Fiction, thoughts and more on Ian RobertS' eclectic time travelling world visit: www.scipio6.wixsite.com/the-wardrobe-door or keep up with his latest tweets @IRobertS_author

#TheWardrobeDoor

Coming soon: Taken Things

Book 1 of Tales From

The Unnatural History Museum

For DAS, my strong female lead.

Eve

The two young women at the station greeted each other with pensive nods. Though they had never met, each knew the presence of the other meant they were both in pretty deep.

'Polly Nightingale?' began the taller girl, lean and sandy-haired, her jeans and down jacket discordant against the other's mid-century dress and overcoat.

'You must be Eve Wells?' replied the brunette, gaze wary above freckle dappled features. Eve returned a discombobulated smile as behind her the guard's whistle blew. Less than ten minutes ago she had been kissing her fiancé goodbye on the edge of campus, yet now she stood amid the steam and bustle of a crowded Scottish railway station at some point in time she couldn't quite fathom. A man in a fedora frowned at her over the top of his *Edinburgh Standard* and she glanced away nervously, yet Polly Nightingale seemed more concerned with the headline of his newspaper: *Monster Fever Grips Caledonia Once Again*. Her brows knotted. 'Things must have become pretty serious if she's brought you along as consultant ...'

Eve looked away. In her every-day life she taught palaeontology at a Midlands university and the very fact she'd been called upon could only have one logical conclusion. It took every ounce of effort to keep her mind from drifting to the memory of the last time she'd been contacted – the crazy events which had turned her understanding of reality upside down.

'She's not here yet?'

'You know what she's like!' Polly grinned and they shared a conspiratorial smile. Though strangers, they were linked by an unspoken secret, mutual acquaintances of the most truly remarkable person. 'Here, let me give you my number, it'd be good to catch up after ...'

'Yeah,' Eve agreed, '- is it right you both ..?'

From what she had learned from their mutual friend, Polly worked at a prestigious London museum, yet her curatorial role had become a doorway to something entirely more incredible.

The girl inclined her head, her expression watchful. 'Best not talk about that now.'

With a nod they stepped behind the nearest pillar, discreetly shielding the glow of their screens from two mothers with perambulators and a gang of workmen packing up for the day.

'Tut-tut ladies,' said a disapproving voice and Eve whisked around to see a diminutive dark- haired figure dressed in vintage hiking gear. 'I see you cannot separate yourselves from your devices - will I need to confiscate them?'

Eve felt a host of memories clamour within her. It had been almost a year since the enigmatic speaker had invaded her life, yet still she had the power to unsettle her. 'All good Dinosaur Girl?'

Eve nodded hesitantly.

Classically beautiful, Ravenna Friere looked like any other confident twenty-five year old, but, as Eve reflected with a sinking feeling, the dark haired woman was anything but. 'I'm sure you can imagine the consequences of this kind of technology being noticed? We are here to untangle chronological problems, not create them!'

Eve cleared her throat as she pocketed her phone, her gaze drawn out across the platform, now thronged with smartly dressed school children; a businessmen tapping out his briar pipe glanced up to meet her gaze. Would any of them ever suspect where they had come from – or how archaic the dark haired girl was? She glanced back to Ravenna. With her flawless Mediterranean complexion and unusual accent they would probably take her for a tourist dressed for a week in the mountains. She looked down at her own clothes and took a step back behind the pillar. 'Where are we?' she ventured, sure the businessman was still watching.

'Later,' the Mediterranean girl replied, 'and as you know well, the question is not where, but *when* ...' She broke off to look her up and down disapprovingly, 'we must get you into something less conspicuous Wells.' And handing her a satchel of clothes gestured towards the ladies conveniences.

Ten minutes later Eve emerged looking like something from a vintage railway poster advertising bracing outings in the country. 'We must do something with your hair,' commented Ravenna, and with Polly's help began to force it into some approximation of mid-twentieth century style. Eve admired herself in Polly's compact, then glanced down at her feet and grimaced.

'Where the hell did you get these hiking boots, the torture chamber at Warwick Castle?'

'No complaining,' the dark-haired girl frowned, 'we have important work to do.'

'So what's the gig?'

The Mediterranean girl hesitated before turning towards the exit.

'We are three school chums on a jolly girls' get-together near the Moray Firth,' Ravenna replied over her shoulder, 'off for a spot of Highland air.'

'But I thought we were taking the sleeper?' Polly frowned, with a glance at the waiting locomotive.

'Things are moving rapidly,' the dark haired girl replied as they descended the steps, 'faster than I could have envisaged - and we must make up for lost time.'

'*Lost time* – but ...' the words died on Eve's lips. A small motor car was awaiting them, parked with a couple of others across the street.

'Austin Seven,' the Mediterranean girl said curtly, 'we can travel direct and non-stop - no connections to make nor time-consuming hikes into the sticks once we get there.'

'Do you want me to drive?' ventured Polly, making for the driver's door as if this was standard procedure.

'Do you know how to double-declutch Nightingale girl?'

Polly seemed to hesitate, then shrugged and took the front passenger seat as Eve headed for the rear with her satchel of modern clothes. 'Do you want me to stick this bag in the boot?'

'No,' Ravenna said sharply, 'I would not open the trunk here – not unless you want to cause ... something of a stir.'

'*O-kay*,' Eve replied slowly, and throwing the bag on the leather seats got in and began looking for a seatbelt.

'I would tell you to buckle up,' Ravenna said with a grin, 'but there are no lap belts - they will not be mandatory until 1983 ...' Eve noticed Polly Nightingale smile wryly, and knowing they would get along well sat back as Ravenna moved jerkily into the traffic.

Hell it was unreal – yet somehow every time the enigmatic Mediterranean girl called her back into the past she managed to adjust. She sighed, knowing it ought not to be possible, but as she lost herself in the long-dead world beyond the window knew that it clearly was.

'Now Nightingale,' the Mediterranean girl continued, 'your phone – we need some banging tunes for the journey.'

Road Trip

Within fifty minutes they were bumping along country lanes, heading out of the city into bigger countryside to a soundtrack of upbeat dance music.

The scenery made Eve's head spin: beautiful, unspoilt, *archaic*. It was time for the hay harvest and men in cloth caps and neckerchiefs were rigging up strange looking machines to shire horses ready for the cut. In the front, Ravenna gunned the engine like a rally-driver, squeezing every ounce of grip out of the thin tyres as she raced along the winding roads.

'Seriously, you're not using up my battery playing house music!' Polly was complaining as the time traveller bobbed her head to the pounding beat, 'what if someone hears us?'

'Who will hear us with these puny speakers Nightingale girl?' Ravenna returned incredulously.

Eve cleared her throat, suddenly desperate to make sense of the crazy road-trip she had found herself on.

'So where *are* we going?'

Ravenna glanced at her in the rear view mirror.

'A body of water between Fort Augusta and Drumnadrochit.'

She nodded and they carried on in silence for a long time, the scenery becoming steeper and more mountainous as they passed into a wooded valley.

'And what are we going to do at this *body of water*?'

'Always questions!' replied Ravenna, while Polly smiled to herself. Eve sat back and turned her attention to the window. Perhaps it was better she didn't know – after all, her specialism could only mean one thing – yet after a while Ravenna relented. 'We are going fishing Eve Wells – or perhaps I should say hunting. This deep ocean inlet is twenty miles long, ample room for a large aquatic animal to hide in – hence the legends which have grown up around the place.'

'*Legends?*' she frowned. Then the penny dropped. 'Oh - you're kidding me!'

'Read this,' said Polly, passing her a sheet of A4.

The Loch Ness Monster - a fairly exhaustive history of the legend printed off from Wikipedia. She scanned it with growing incredulity. She'd heard of the story since childhood but had never really given it any serious thought. As she read the long list of accounts and sightings a feeling of concern began to tug at her gut.

'I have spoken before of places where the weave of time pulls tightly,' Ravenna continued, 'and even touches – *close places* – and it has been bought to my attention that *this* is such a place.'

An almost Nordic scene had opened up before them, steep mountains soaring high above an immense steel-grey stretch of water. Eve nodded pensively. She still couldn't get her head around the fact that time was not a line but a knotted tangle, yet their very presence in this place was living proof. 'I believe the fissure in the temporal weave has happened only a handful of times before in this place.'

Eve glanced down at the sheet. 'Like when St. Columba defeated the monster with the sign of the cross in AD565.'

'And when Donald Mackenzie of Balnain saw the monster in 1871,' Polly added, realisation clearly dawning, '… which would explain why there have been so few sightings.'

Ravenna nodded, her gaze fixed hawk-like on the road. 'Indeed - the rift here is clearly cyclical, and ever since George Spicer saw the monster in 1933 – this very year – it has happened roughly every decade: Peter MacNab's famous 1955 photograph and sonar readings, Tim Dinsdale's film of a wake across the Loch in the 60's, Anthony Shiel's '77 photo of a long-necked creature and so on.'

Polly nodded seriously. 'With six sightings between 1933 and '38 something is clearly going on at this particular point in time.'

Eve frowned. They were passing a wooded stretch near the water's edge. 'This section of road is the very one on which

George Spicer and his wife allegedly saw "a most extraordinary form of animal" crossing the road in front of their car, they claimed it had a body around four feet high and twenty five in length, it's neck long and ...' She broke off as Polly yelped unexpectedly, and looking up saw the last thing she had ever expected to see. 'Oh, and here it is!' Ravenna added in a matter-of-fact tone as Eve's heart leapt out of her chest, her stomach lurching wildly as Ravenna threw the wheel hard right, sending the car skidding towards the grass verge.

She twisted her head as she grabbed the back of Polly's seat. A mound of grey flesh - elephant-like at first glance, but more whale-like on reflection - a cracked yet blubbery mass - was lumbering across the metalled road with the undulating motion of an elephant seal.

'Holy ..!

The car struck the verge with a disconcerting lurch, making them scream as they ricocheted past the creature's vanishing tail, before coming to an abrupt halt against the bank. Ravenna was out in a flash. 'Did you see it Wells, did you get a clear glimpse?'

Eve was nursing a bruised shoulder.

'I – yes, but I don't really ...'

Ravenna scowled at her darkly. 'Brilliant, *Dinosaur Girl,* that was maybe our only chance to identify it in daylight!' She threw open the door and Eve stumbled out to gaze desperately at the swaying foliage left in its wake. There was nothing but an eerie silence now as if the woods were holding their breath.

'Must be its regular run,' Polly mused, glancing at the deep gouges and flattened foliage.

Eve nodded. 'The latest research seems to suggest many aquatic dinosaurs came to nest on land at night …' she broke off, hardly able to believe what she was saying.

'Come,' said Ravenna grimly, 'we are in the right place – now, roll up your sleeves, we must move this car …' But Eve hardly heard, still staring at the place the creature had disappeared.

'Woah - I've just seen the Loch Ness Monster.'

The Guest House

'Not hungry ladies?'

Polly and Eve glanced at each other as Ravenna calmly shovelled poached egg into her mouth. Food was the last thing on Eve's mind, she felt homesick and mildly nauseous. 'Well, waste not, want not!' Ravenna continued, reaching for Eve's plate.

Eve turned her attention to the view beyond the net curtains. The guesthouse stood next to a vicarage a stone's throw from the Loch - the perfect base from which to explore its brooding waters. She shuddered. It seemed almost impossible that it had once sat beneath a primeval ocean – the ocean from which the monster had no doubt come.

'So Eve Wells, your professional verdict?'

She looked up briskly, shooting Ravenna an anxious glance. 'On what we saw?'

'Yes, Dinosaur Girl,' the dark haired girl replied impatiently, 'of the creature by the loch.'

Eve hesitated. 'A plesiosaur of some kind – *elasmosaurus* ... *cryptoclidus*? There are at least twenty species of long-necked *sauropterygians* which would fit the bill.' She broke off as both women looked at her blankly, but was saved the trouble of elaborating by the appearance of Mrs McLeod, the proprietor, who entered to clear away the plates.

'All finished there girls? Would you be wanting the wireless on in the sitting room?'

'No, thank you,' Ravenna replied primly in a neat Oxbridge accent, 'would it be possible to have some more tea?'

The woman nodded and left the room.

'But I thought the classic monster sightings had been dismissed as hoaxes?' Eve ventured once she had gone, 'the long-neck-out-of-the-water picture at least – a plesiosaur could never extend its neck directly upwards like that ...'

Ravenna shrugged. 'Something is in this Loch and I now firmly believe it is a chronological anomaly ...' She broke off as the door opened again. To Eve's surprise it was not Mrs McLeod: a tall young man stood in the doorway in a dark suit and dog-collar.

'Oh, sorry ladies,' he said apologetically, 'I had no idea there were guests still breakfasting.'

'No problem,' said Eve instinctively. Polly added:

'Don't mind us!'

'No, of course ...' he replied bashfully, 'I'm James Roberts – the curate of St Mary's- I was just calling on Mrs McLeod ...'

'Cool,' smiled Eve without thinking. The young man frowned.

'Right, well, I'll be getting along now - parishioners to visit and all that ...'

'Have a good day,' said Ravenna neatly. The young man nodded awkwardly then left the room.

'*Hashtag hot vicar,*' grinned Polly after a moment and they all laughed.

'*Cool,*' tutted Ravenna with a disapproving inclination of her eyebrows. 'That term will not be used widely for at least another sixty years! Now children – down to business.'

A thoughtful hush fell.

'So, we have some idea what we are up against,' Polly ventured, sipping her tea, 'but in the deepest stretch of inland waterway in the UK - which as you said is over twenty miles long - how on earth are we going to find a creature the size of an elephant?'

'A small whale,' Eve corrected but Polly ignored her.

'Simple,' Ravenna replied with a matter-of-fact inclination of her eyebrows, 'bait – we find its favourite food.'

'*Which is?*' Polly challenged.

Ravenna smiled and made a gesture towards Eve with her fork.

'Ammonites?'

'*Boom*,' the dark haired girl smiled, 'and this, Eve Wells, is why I have brought you!'

*

'This plan is sheer simplicity,' Ravenna was saying as they unloaded an assortment of duffle bags from the car.

Eve looked on nervously, dreading that the landlady or some guest would appear and start asking questions. 'We go out onto the Loch at night and take a dive. We use our abilities to open a rift to the Mesozoic seas, we allow through some smaller aquatic fauna of the sort a plesiosaur would love, use it to attract the *monster*, then usher it back and seal the rift.'

'So simple,' replied Polly glibly, 'no danger involved at all.' Ravenna shrugged.

'If you have any better ideas Nightingale ..?' But Eve interrupted before she could reply.

'What? You're going to *dive* in Loch Ness? But it's connected to the Moray Firth – it's practically deep ocean!'

'I have few other options,' Ravenna returned darkly, then broke off as footfalls crunched on the gravel behind her.

'Ladies,' said the young curate they had met earlier. They smiled back warmly at the passing man, Polly giving a friendly wave; but as she did so the canvas bag she was unloading fell open and a scuba hose slipped out onto the gravel. Eve felt the breath catch in her throat as the young man's eyes darted to it, Polly moving swiftly to push it back in, while Ravenna cursed under her breath. 'Well, I'll be on my way,' the young man continued briskly, and to their relief hurried off towards the village.

'So what now?' asked Eve a little shakily.

'We take a hike,' Ravenna replied tersely, 'and find a place to dive.'

The Loch

Eve massaged her aching feet dejectedly.

'Much as I like the outdoors, we've spent hours walking and haven't heard of a single monster sighting.'

They were perched on a timeworn landing stage, gazing out over the mirror-like surface of the water. Ravenna seemed not to hear, staring stoically across the Loch at the castle which shimmered in the late-morning air. The Mediterranean girl frowned then glanced back to the guest house behind them, its ivy clad walls just visible barely twenty yards up the lane.

'This place is as good as any,' she mused quietly, 'now all we need ...'

She broke off, and Eve glanced up sharply as a dark shape appeared on the water, moving steadily towards them from the east about twenty yards out. Eve felt her scalp prickle, but as she stared on in silence the shape became more distinct: a rowing boat with a single occupant.

'*Magna Mater*,' Ravenna muttered then stood to watch the approaching vessel.

As the boat came alongside the jetty, a grizzled man in his sixties glanced up at them with interest, nodding curtly as he threw up the rope.

'So you're the three lassies hunting monsters are ye?'

'Oh – yes, we – erm …' Eve replied awkwardly, but Ravenna interrupted with a confident smile.

'We're just up for a weekend's hiking,' she interjected calmly in a prim tone, 'fresh air and wide open spaces.'

The old man looked up at her sceptically then began to unload a rod and tackle. 'You's been asking a lot of questions about monsters for three young ladies who aren't particularly interested in monsters.'

Eve shot Polly a concerned look.

'Fresh mountain air and fair prospects are all we're here for,' Ravenna continued, 'and if we happen to bump into a monster, then all the better.'

The old man inclined his head and made a sound in his throat which may have been a chuckle. It certainly seemed unlikely: three young women alone in the wilds hunting mythical creatures. Eve felt her heart sinking. 'You're reporters aren't ye?' he added as he climbed up onto the jetty, 'newspaper types from London up for a story …'

'I couldn't possibly comment,' Ravenna replied with an evasive smile. The old man shook his head wryly.

'Well, I've been fishing this Loch for nigh-on forty years and have nare seen hide n' hair of any beast, metaphysical or otherwise.'

Ravenna returned a pert smile then glanced at his tethered boat. 'Well perhaps we'll get lucky … we'll give you ten bob if you leave your boat here tonight and turn a blind eye, twice as much if we get a photograph.'

The fisherman shouldered his rod and looked at her levelly. Ravenna dug in her back pocket. A smile cracked the old man's lips and he nodded, extending his hand.

'But don't go making a song-and-dance about it will ye now, for the bailiffs are devilish keen on feeling a poacher's collar – if you get my meaning.'

'We certainly won't,' the Mediterranean girl replied demurely. The man raised a hand in farewell then went on his way.

Eve glanced at her sceptically. 'So let me get this straight: this is really happening - we're about to try and catch the Loch Ness Monster?'

Ravenna turned towards the guest house gesturing to Polly and with a sigh Eve followed.

Encounter

It was pitch dark after the brightness of their room and Eve's eyes struggled to adjust. It was overcast – a moonless night – and the mountains seemed to glower down upon the valley draining all colour from the land.

'Come on,' said Polly squeezing her arm, 'let's get this over with before Mrs McLeod wakes up and finds us sneaking out.'

Ravenna appeared at her side. 'You two finish getting the kit ready and I'll make sure the old man has been good to his word.' She dumped a bag on the gravel with an overly loud crunch then disappeared, leaving them to sort the dive gear. Eve shook her head in disbelief. It was madness.

'Right, I'd better get set,' sighed Polly, and taking her wetsuit headed for the shelter of the garden wall. Eve shivered as she contemplated what lay ahead, her eyes lingering on the ink black loch, but then, unexpectedly, Polly hissed a warning.

She jerked her gaze towards the drive and to her horror saw light flare.

'*Hey!* You there ..!'

She turned briskly to find herself staring into the worried face of James Roberts. 'This must stop now,' the torch wielding curate said shakily, 'I don't know what you're up to, but I'm calling the police – I knew there was something rum about you from the first – your strange turn of phrase and the fantastical gear in your car – I'm putting a stop to this nonsense right away!'

'Please!' she whispered back but he took no heed.

'I've heard what's happening in Germany … voices saying there may be another war …' he took a shaky breath, 'you're spies aren't you, foreigners gathering information!'

'No!' said Eve desperately, 'you've got it wrong!'

'You're coming with me,' he continued firmly, taking her arm, '– and your friend who's hiding behind the wall!'

Eve felt panic grip her, watching helplessly as Polly stood slowly, but as she did so, a shadow rushed out of the darkness and the clergyman crumpled unexpectedly.

'Forgive me Father for I have sinned,' Ravenna Friere whispered in a tone which left Eve unsure if it were ironic or sincere, and promptly began dragging the unconscious clergyman behind the wall. 'Well, what are you waiting for? Let's go!'

Eve just stared, but the Mediterranean girl seemed not to notice.

'Put this on,' said Ravenna, handing her the down jacket she'd taken off at the station, 'just keep calm and try to relax.'

'*Relax!* she shot back incredulously, 'You've just knocked out a vicar! And I can't wear this! What if someone sees us – you heard what he said! Hell, if anyone finds us here with all this stuff - there's kit here which could change the outcome of the Second World War, the entire shape of the future!'

'Put the damned jacket on,' said Ravenna firmly, 'you are panicking Wells – it will be cold on the Loch.'

She hesitated, then consented, struggling to keep her gaze from where the young man lay.

The Loch Again

Ten minutes later they sat enveloped in darkness, bobbing on the brooding surface of the Loch about fifteen metres from the shore. Eve shuddered. Their tiny boat seemed dwarfed by the vastness of the landscape. Ravenna looked resolute but there was something unsettled in her dark expression.

'Anything we should know Wells?'

Eve glanced anxiously at the waves which lapped against the boat. 'The early Cretaceous oceans were vast and tropical – sea levels were at least three hundred feet higher and there were tons of reefs; less land mass than today - you'll be pretty deep.' Polly nodded pensively. 'And the Mesozoic Marine Revolution meant the arrival of modern fish – and predators to feed on them, loads of big creatures like plesiosaurs and pliosaurs ...' She broke off seeing Polly's expression darken.

'Our thanks for your heartening words,' Ravenna said grimly, before ducking down to busy herself with her dive kit.

'Sorry,' Eve whispered apologetically. Polly's face was ghostly white against her wetsuit, her eyes unnaturally large. She returned a weak smile as she perched her diving mask on the top of her head. 'You okay?'

'Not really – I'm terrified of deep water – and this is my second ever dive.'

'Oh,' Eve replied awkwardly.

'Hay-ho,' the museum curator shrugged, 'I've got to do this, it's only me and Ravenna who can …' Eve nodded appreciatively, still hardly able to believe what was about to happen, then squeezed her shoulder reassuringly.

'All ready?' Ravenna whispered loudly. Polly gave Eve a reassuring look and with a nod they put in their regulators and dropped backwards over the side.

Polly

Polly forced herself to breathe evenly as the frigid waters engulfed her, an abyss of gloom and muffled noise containing god-only-knew-what horrors. It took every ounce of self-control to keep her head, following as Ravenna kicked downwards, out and away from the boat, the pressure building slowly as they descended through silt and streaming bubbles. She scanned the gloom anxiously, wary of every shape and movement, expecting at any moment for some primeval thing to manifest itself before her mask. The horror of it seemed to crawl around her, the sheer stupidity and the danger, the water like a living presence pressing down from every side.

She tried to focus her mind on Ravenna's kicking fins. The dark-haired girl seemed to be quickening her pace, pushing deeper as they spiralled into the darkness. She tried not to gulp her air as she struggled to keep up, but Ravenna - by far the stronger swimmer - was pulling ahead; and with a stab of concern she began to kick harder, concentrating on her stroke, forcing herself not to check her depth gauge. When would she deem it deep enough?

Her thighs were aching now, muscles burning as she began to gain, yet just as she drew level with Ravenna, something surged out of the darkness to her right. She gasped, jerking back instinctively, twisting in a panicked stream of bubbles – only to see a large fish flash away into the blackness. Dizzy with relief she skulled for a moment then looked down with concern. Ravenna was already far below her, seemingly oblivious. She followed with a desperate kick of her fins, descending into the emptiness, further and further from the apparent safety of the boat; but at last the time traveller slowed and turned, gesturing that it was time. Polly took a breath, hardly able to believe the ancient secret she had been drawn into, then replied with a nod.

Drawing strength from the confidence in the other girl's eyes she focussed her mind as Ravenna raised her hands. Almost instantly, living shadows seemed to writhe and deepen, swirling and arcing outwards to twist and fuse. A pool of inky solidity shimmered before them and with a nod Ravenna bid her swim into it. She held her breath as darkness surrounded her, then gasped as it gave way to light.

The temperature was changing, growing discernibly warmer. A hazy tropical light filtered down from the surface high above: the Mesozoic ocean. A searing headache lanced unexpectedly across her forehead and Polly had to fight to stay upright. For a moment she panicked, but with a rush of relief felt Ravenna grip her shoulder. She tried to breathe evenly through her regulator - just her brain adjusting to the titanic shift in time it had experienced - she made the *okay* gesture and the dark-haired girl continued with a nod.

They swam for fifteen minutes or so, seeing nothing but silvery fish and jellies, then headed up towards the light. Breaking the surface Polly began to scan desperately for any sight of land.

'*My god!*'

They were in an ocean, miles from shore, the white sand of tropical islands just visible below swaying palms. 'This is incredible!'

Polly took a breath to clear her head. They were bobbing amid powerful waves, salt stinging her lips as strange sounds swirled on the warm breeze - the call of long dead things - but Ravenna seemed unmoved.

'What are those?' she said impatiently, then putting in her regulator ducked beneath the waves. Polly frowned. It took a moment for her to realise what the strange shapes bobbing a few yards ahead were, and with a gasp of excitement pulled down her mask and followed.

Ammonites - the iconic spiral-shelled marine creature - some bobbing serenely while others jetted swiftly with explosive squid-like expulsions of bubbles. She floated for a moment, mesmerised, aware that she was seeing something generations of scientists had longed to see. There was a tap on her shoulder and Ravenna made a stabbing gesture with her finger: *go grab one*. She replied with a nod. They rounded on the creature slowly, trying not to disturb the water with their fins, but as Polly got within a couple of feet it sensed the other woman and jetted away making her jerk back violently.

Ravenna scowled behind her mask. *Try again.*

Another ammonite – about the size of a car tyre - bobbed a couple of metres above them. She skulled forward gently, extending her hand towards the seemingly docile creature. It did not move. A thought struck her and she began to wriggle her fingers gently, imitating some passing sea creature. With a surge of triumph she saw its squid like tentacles begin to emerge, dipping gently from the aperture at the base of the spiral. Ravenna gave her an approving nod, her hands almost closed around the shell. She was grinning as she wriggled her fingers closer, knowing the hardest part was now over, but then – to her horror – the gently waving tentacles shot forward to latch themselves around her hand with a horrifying grip. She cried out instinctively, wrenching her hand away with an impulsive jerk, realising her mistake too late as her respirator blew free in a blinding explosion of bubbles.

She spiralled, flailing wildly, trying to shake the powerful creature from her hand, clamping her mouth closed as her lungs began to burn. She kicked and punched as panic overwhelmed her, the vice-like grip crushing the bones in her fingers as she fought the instinct to take a breath. Her vision blurred - the world a chaos of turquoise and silver bubbles - and then the regulator was being pushed into her mouth, the grip on her hand vanishing almost instantly as a familiar pair of eyes looked firmly into hers.

Swim up, gestured Ravenna. She had the ammonite tucked under her arm like a parcel and a knife in her right hand.

Polly fought not to sob as she pushed up her mask to examine her fingers: they were badly bruised and cut in several places, the wounds stinging fiercely. She had almost drowned and the shock was beginning to make her tremble.

'Come on,' the Mediterranean girl said gently, 'well done Nightingale girl.'

She nodded weakly, wiping saltwater from her face as she struggled with the pain in her hand. Above them large shapes where wheeling, the air filled with the unearthly cries of circling pterosaurs - but there was little time to contemplate them. 'We have what we came for - now for the hard part.'

Great.

She nodded, and dropping her gaze to the living fossil in the other girl's hand pulled down her mask.

Monster

There were lights moving on the shore, the sound of shouting and the barking of dogs carrying clearly across the stillness of the loch.

Eve swore and flattened herself against the bottom of the boat as torch beams lanced overhead. She gritted her teeth, heart pounding, wrinkling her nose at the smell of stagnant water. What the hell was she going to do? A voice was calling out, bellowing loudly, but she couldn't make out the words. Where were they? She fought panic. Their chances of bringing back an ammonite as bait seemed suddenly more than ludicrous. She paused for a moment longer, her heart thudding, then, daring to glance up, saw the last thing she had ever expected.

Her heart missed a beat, the lights completely forgotten. A dark shape was moving with surprising swiftness across the black surface of the loch ahead of her, its white V-like wake clearly visible in the gloom.

'*Oh god!*'

Eve swore as she realised what she was seeing, some primeval instinct screaming at her to escape – but there was nowhere to go. The head broke the surface ten yards from the boat, huge liquid eyes and finger-length spines of teeth like an angler-fish. A strangled noise gurgled inside her throat but she was frozen, paralysed with terror as the creature closed on her. The calls from the shore became a distant blur.

She felt suddenly detached, her mind seeming to baulk at the impossibility of what she was seeing, longing for it to be some crazy dream. Yet there it was, the smooth ridge of its spine now visible, its broad muzzle opening and closing as it eyed her. An odd part of her felt she ought to be fascinated, to note some scientific observation, but she felt only primal terror, the utter horror of a creature which could end her life.

Eight yards away … seven yards. It was heading straight for the boat, eyes glistening.

Cold sweat broke and trickled down her back, her fingers aching from where they gripped the seat so tightly. Hell, these things were supposed to be fish eaters – perhaps it thought the boat was a rival male?

It moved almost silently – with a dreadful yet serene predictability – six yards … five. It was going to ram the boat and pitch her into the icy blackness. She ducked and screamed, then driven by some instinct she didn't quite understand made the sign of the cross as she screwed her eyes firmly shut.

*

Polly broke the surface with a gasp, scanning desperately, disoriented by the shift from tropical day to Caledonian night.

For a second she couldn't place the boat and panic flared, but then she saw it, a dark shape about seven yards away, stark against the hills. She sensed Ravenna at her side and with a nod they swam briskly towards it – but as she did so became aware of an anxious voice calling from the vessel.

'It's here!' hissed Eve as she put her arm over the side, 'it's in the water … I … I made the sign of the cross and …'

'Like St Columba,' Ravenna said thoughtfully as she hauled the ammonite up into the boat. '*Deo Gracias!*'

'My god!' Eve replied as she saw the huge mollusc, 'is that ..!'

'Yes, but it is dead,' Ravenna said curtly, 'Nightingale forced me to dispatch it.' Polly felt too weak to reply. Her hand was aching fiercely, her head swimming with the pain. Then realisation struck her: *it's in the water!*

She gasped, the urge to climb into the boat near overwhelming, but even as she thought it, a beam of light washed over them. She froze instinctively. Lights were blazing in the cottage, whistles blaring. She heard Eve swear under her breath.

'What if they put a boat out - we've got to get out of here!'

36

But Ravenna seemed unmoved by the commotion. 'Nightingale – find out where the monster is!'

'*What?*'

'Just do it Nightingale girl!'

She knew there was no other option. Pulling down her mask with trembling hands she ducked beneath the surface and was met almost instantly by the sight of a swift moving flipper about the size of a car door. She panicked, sculling away in a flurry of bubbles and breaking the surface grabbed desperately for the side of the boat.

'Well, is it there?' Ravenna asked angrily. She nodded dumbly, feeling hysteria begin to tug at her as she desperately clutched the bulwark. She needed to get out of the water, needed to get away … a dark shape broke the surface a few yards to their rear and she yelped in synchrony with Eve.

From the shore more torch beams were scanning the surface of the loch and they ducked instinctively as painful light fell across the boat once more. 'What the hell are we going to do?'

Ravenna took a shaky breath, then gritting her teeth said: 'Pass me the ammonite Wells - I'll lure it down and close the gap!'

Polly stared at her incredulously, disbelief momentarily overriding her fear. 'But how the hell …' She would have to do it from the inside – from the Mesozoic.

'You must stay with Eve – get her out of here – back to her home!'

'You can't …' she stammered, 'I'll come with you …'

But Ravenna had already slipped in her regulator and was disappearing in a flurry of fins.

'Go after her!' Eve gasped wide-eyed, but Polly found herself unable to release the side of the boat, horribly aware of the thing which still eyed her from the stern.

'I –,' she began, but then the monster vanished abruptly and with a jolt of realisation she knew she had to follow. Shoving in her regulator she twisted forwards and with a pounding heart propelled herself into the gloom.

At first there were bubbles, the clear sign of movement, but after a moment they began to fade. She dived deeper, the pressure pushing at her chest, but there was now no sign of either Ravenna or the creature. She swam and swam, the blackness pressing down on her for what seemed like hours, and then, remembering her air tank, checked her gauge and with a sting of concern kicked sadly upwards.

'Ravenna?' asked Eve as she grasped the side of the boat.

Polly pushed back her mask and clawed at the tears which stung her eyes. Eve took a breath and began to haul her in.

'She must have done something,' the fair-haired girl said quietly as Polly struggled into the boat, 'I got this headache - about ten minutes after you went after her – and when I looked up the shore was deserted.'

Following her gaze Polly saw that the lights along the shore had indeed gone. She took a breath to calm herself and pulled back the hood of her wetsuit.

'She must have done it – she must have changed time - lured it to the Mesozoic and closed the rift.'

Eve nodded hopefully. 'No monster, so no monster-craze, so no reporters – just three crazy school friends on holiday in the Highlands.' Polly swallowed away a lump in her throat.

'Two friends.'

Eve looked at her, then cuffed at her eyes.

'Do you think she'll be okay?'

Polly forced herself to be resolute. 'She *has* been dead before,' she said with a melancholy smile, '- hell, this is insane!'

Eve gave her a hug then began to help her out of her buoyancy jacket.

She must be out there – *surely*. If she had died in the past they would never even know that she existed - they never would have met. The thought was almost too much to process. She took a shaky breath. Even after all this time she still had no idea who Ravenna really was or how she did what she did. A girl who had long ago slipped through a door in time? A phantom, or perhaps - as she had once thought– an angel? She glanced down at her aching hand. She still had no clue whether what she could do was science, magic or a miracle.

'So what now?'

Eve seemed trapped between horror and relief. They were just two girls alone in a boat. It could have been any time.

Polly shrugged. 'Now The Loch Ness Monster really *is* just a myth … I get you home. We keep in touch - we wait …'

Eve nodded. 'We wait until she contacts us again – wait until she calls on us.'

Polly smiled sadly. 'Until the next time.' She focussed her mind, watching fascinated as dark tendrils of mist began to writhe across her palm.

Eve Wells closed her eyes. "Til next time …'

Acknowledgments

Deeper Realms wouldn't be possible without the help, encouragement, love and support of: Deborah Storer, John Green, Penelope Wallace, Clare Portwood, Simone Greenwood and everyone else who has given me both the physical and mental space to create the world which Ravenna Friere inhabits.

Printed in Great Britain
by Amazon

86410938R00025